MY WORDS FLEW AWAY LIKE BIRDS

For all the families who come to North York Central Library in Toronto, especially those children who come here from far away — D.P.

For Mom — S.J.

Special thanks to Yoojin Kwon and Laleh Moshiri for their careful reading of the text and their thoughtful feedback.

Published in Canada and the U.S. by Kids Can Press Ltd.
25 Dockside Drive, Toronto, ON M5A 0B5

Kids Can Press is a Corus Entertainment Inc. company

www.kidscanpress.com

The artwork and hand-lettering in this book were created in pen and ink, with color added digitally.
The text is set in Colby.
Hand-lettering by Shrija Jain.

Edited by Yasemin Uçar
Designed by Andrew Dupuis

Printed and bound in Heyuan, China, in 03/2021 by Asia Pacific Offset

CM 21 0 9 8 7 6 5 4 3 2 1

Library and Archives Canada Cataloguing in Publication

Title: My words flew away like birds / Debora Pearson ; [illustrated by] Shrija Jain.
Names: Pearson, Debora, author. | Jain, Shrija, 1993- illustrator.
Identifiers: Canadiana 20200388193 | ISBN 9781525303180 (hardcover)
Classification: LCC PS8581.E383 M9 2021 | DDC jC813/.6 — dc23

Kids Can Press gratefully acknowledges that the land on which our office is located is the traditional territory of many nations, including the Mississaugas of the Credit, the Anishnabeg, the Chippewa, the Haudenosaunee and the Wendat peoples, and is now home to many diverse First Nations, Inuit and Métis peoples.

We thank the Government of Ontario, through Ontario Creates; the Ontario Arts Council; the Canada Council for the Arts; and the Government of Canada for supporting our publishing activity.

MY WORDS FLEW AWAY LIKE BIRDS

DEBORA PEARSON
SHRIJA JAIN

KIDS CAN PRESS

Before I came here,
I could see the world
from my bedroom window.

ALL
THE
PLACES
I KNEW,

the homes of my friends,
the trees we ran under
on our way to school
and the noisy market
where I went shopping
with my mother and aunts.

My favorite part of the market
was my grandfather's bakery
where everything,
especially my grandfather,
smelled like

FRESH,
WARM
BREAD.

That was my world
back then.

Before we moved away,
my mother taught me
some words in a new language.
She said we would need these words,
and other ones, too,
in the place where we were going.

The words felt strange
and lumpy
in my mouth.

"HELLO, how are you?"

"I am very well,
THANK YOU."

"It was
NICE TO
MEET YOU."

"GOODBYE!"

What would it be like,
I wondered,
to live where
everyone said these words?
And I would, too.

But when we came here,
my mother,
my father
and me,
all my words flew away like birds.

Everyone spoke so fast,
their words TUMBLED OUT AND SWIRLED AROUND.

HEY!
WHAT'S UP?
NOT MUCH.
WHACHADOING?
C'MON, LET'S GO.
SHEESH! WAIT UP.
NAAAAAAA.
OKAY, OKAY.
OOPS! MY BAD.
GOTTA GO.
WHATEVER.
SEE YOU LATER.
YEAH SURE,
MAYBE LATER.

Their words did not sound
like the ones I had learned.
So I did not say anything.
I was like a tiny bug
on a little leaf

WAITING,
WATCHING,
LISTENING,

trying to figure out where I had landed,
trying to fit in.

At school I watched
the teacher's chalk

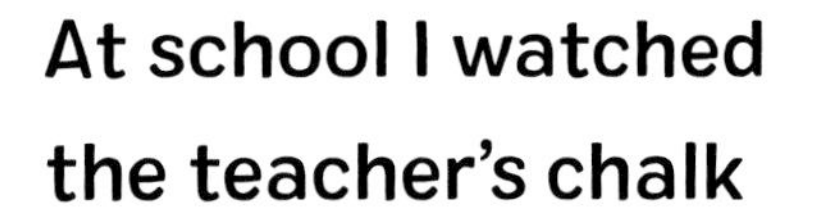

DANCE

across the chalkboard,
making words I did not know.

I listened to sounds
crickle-crackle,

MUMBLE
JUMP
FROM THE
BOX

above the teacher's desk.
A voice said things
I did not understand.

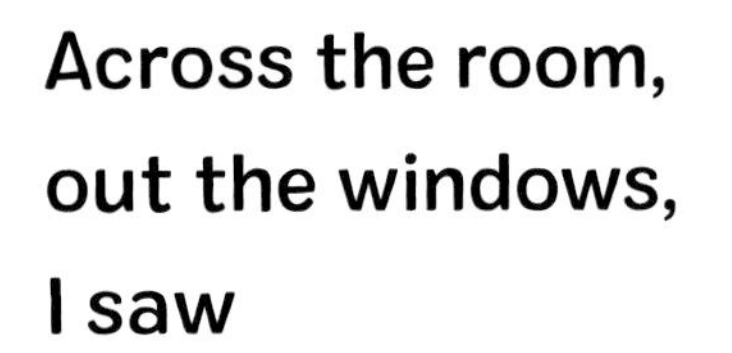

Across the room,
out the windows,
I saw

TREES,
SKY,
A PARK.

But not my trees,
my sky,
my park.
Not the ones I knew.

I wished my friends from back home
were here.

I would have shown them
the snow falling down
and the dog in a coat
and **TINY DOG BOOTS**
playing outside.
I had never seen a dog
like that before.

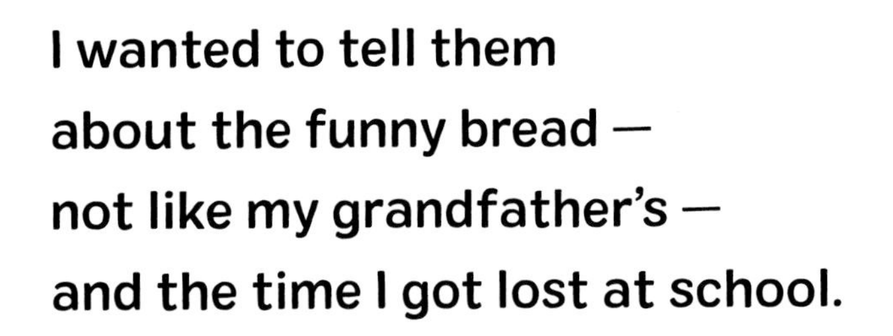

I wanted to tell them
about the funny bread —
not like my grandfather's —
and the time I got lost at school.

The teacher who found me
called me
the NEW

GIRL.

I am not new.
I am just me,
the same as always.
Everything else,
even that teacher,
is New.

One night, Mr. Taggart,
who fixes things in the
tall,
tall
building where we live now,

CLOMP
CLOMP
CLOMPED

down the hall
in big boots
and knocked
on our door.

he said.

We did not know what
“Surprise!”
meant.
Was something broken?

Another

MAN IN BOOTS

stood there, too.

"My assistant," said Mr. Taggart.
"He's from the same place
you folks are.
I'm sure you have lots to talk about."

It took a while for us to understand
Mr. Taggart's words.

He smiled
and waved his hands
like he was conducting

MUSIC.

"Go on!" he said to us.

But when my father spoke to the man
in our old language,
the man did not understand.
He was not from the same place
as us.

Mr. Taggart looked confused.
No one knew what to do.
Finally my mother smiled.
She said to the man
in our shiny new words,

"IT WAS NICE

TO MEET YOU."

The man smiled back.
"It was nice to meet you," he said.

"GOODBYE!"

HE CLOMPED AWAY

with Mr. Taggart,
who still looked confused,
and that was the end
of our
Surprise!

In spring,
when the snow was finally gone,
I went to the park
and walked

DOWN
THE
HILL

to the playground.

A girl wearing a hat
blue as the sky
was there,
nobody else,
swinging up
down up
down up

until she slipped
off
and fell on the ground.
She started to cry.

I did not know what to do.
I picked up her hat.
I brushed it off
and gave it to her.
I tried to think of
something to say.
Then I remembered.
"Hello, how are you?"

The girl wiped her eyes.
"I'm okay," she said.
"Thanks for getting my hat."
She pulled it on
and ran
UP THE HILL
very fast
to someone waiting there.

At the top,
she turned
and waved to me.

"SEE YOU!"

she called.
I waved, too.
"See you!"
I called.
But she was already gone.

This is what happened
the next week at recess.
Everyone else was
running, laughing,
leaping like rabbits,
when I saw
the GIRL WITH THE BLUE HAT!

She ran over
and said,

"YOU
GO HERE?
I DIDN'T KNOW
THAT!"

I said,
"I go here!
I didn't know that!"

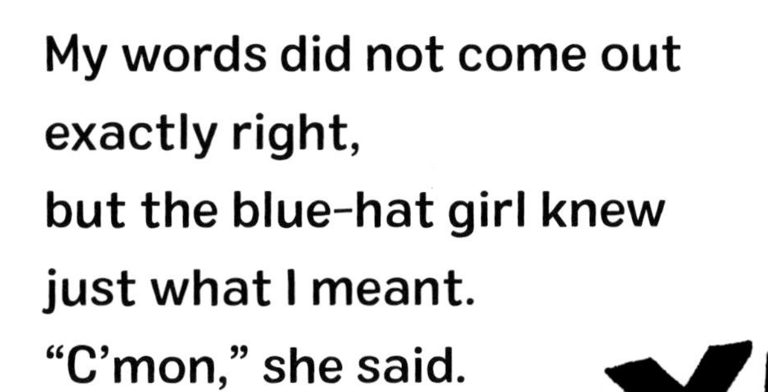

My words did not come out
exactly right,
but the blue-hat girl knew
just what I meant.
"C'mon," she said.

"LET'S PLAY!"

She grabbed my hand
and we ran all over,
laughing and leaping
like rabbits.

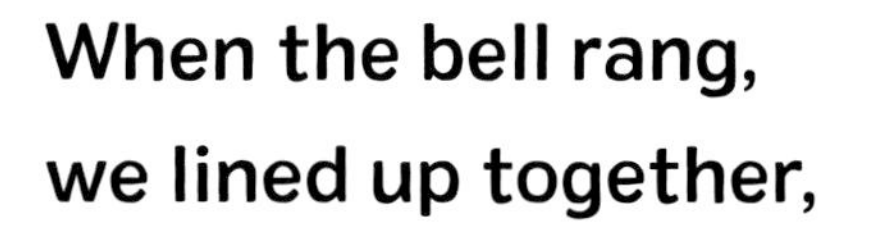

When the bell rang,
we lined up together,

ME AND MY NEW FRIEND,

still holding hands.
We walked to our classrooms.
"See you!"
she said.

“SEE YOU!”

I said.
And this time I knew
I would see her
soon.

When I came here,
all my words flew away.

That was back then.
Now I have new words:

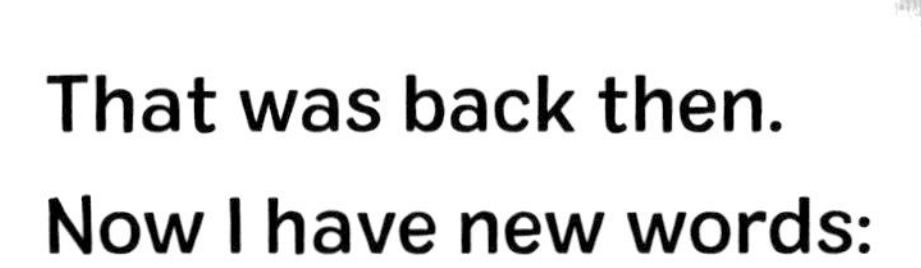

my friend
my baby brother
our home
our trees
our park
our sky ...

And these words
are here
to stay.